Some things
to laugh,
cry
or
talk about

Crumps Barn Studio
No.2 The Waterloo, Cirencester GL7 2PZ
www.crumpsbarnstudio.co.uk

Cover design by Lorna Gray

Printed in the UK by Severn, Gloucester on responsibly sourced paper

MIX
Paper from
responsible sources
FSC® C022174

CARBON NEUTRAL

FSC
www.fsc.org

ISBN 978-1-915067-39-5

Some things *to* laugh, cry *or* talk about

BEVERLEY GORDON

Collected Poems

Crumps Barn Studio

AM I

Am I the only one who finds the night sky beautiful
Am I the only one who loves to hear the
    pitter-patter of raindrops
Am I the only one who thinks life is a journey
If only I could just read that damn map

Am I the only one who thinks the city we live in
    looks beautiful
From far up high, especially set against
    the night light
Am I the only one who looks forward to tomorrow
Even though I really do not know what it will bring
Am I the only one longing for that place
    I love to call
Serenity.

GIVE ME PLEASE

Give me please a place to rest my head
Give me please a place to lay my bed
Give me please a place to call my own
Give me please my favourite meal for the day
Give me please a job so I can get paid
Give me please a helping hand but not today
Give me please time to think of what to say
Give me please your time always.

THANKFUL

Being thankful is never a crime
Being thankful gives me peace of mind
Being thankful helps me to have no regrets
Being thankful for pushing through the hard times
Helps me to know my strengths
Being thankful for the good times
Being thankful not to take life for granted
Being thankful yet for another day.
Always be thankful.

YEARS

Years have come and gone, I continue to
    grow strong
As each day bring on more challenges
A pinch of salt, a little sugar to take the
    bad taste away
Life is not a paradise, it's an obstacle course
A puzzle or a maze
As the years push and pull
You grow old and tired yet still standing
In the same place, now who is to blame?

SO WHAT

So what if I am unhappy
So what if I am sad
So what if my day is not going to plan
So what if my day is too long
So what if I run last in the marathon
So what if I wet my pants
So what if I have no clue as to what to say next
Give it a rest, it's my so what day.

PILLOW TALK

Pillow talk is not for me, shut up and go to sleep
Pillow talk is not for me, let me go and make
    a cup of tea
Pillow talk is not for me, what a time to
    start gossiping
Pillow talk is not for me, I just want to go to sleep
Pillow talk is not for me, just suck two sweets
In fact, fill your mouth, that should keep
    your tongue busy
Please, I need to get some sleep
You have all day to chat but still you wait till
    it's time for bed
What the bleep, I beg you go to sleep
Your mouth is running overtime
I beg you again, let your big mouth have a rest.

MY DEFENCE

In my defence I try my hardest
In my defence I was not taught how to
    read a road map
In my defence the road map stopped at the edge
Turn the page you did not say

In my defence I had to cash the cheque
    I had no cash
In my defence I had to bounce
In my defence I must disagree, a sat nav is
    really not for me
In my defence you have to give up
    chatting about me.

I AM ME

I am not tall I am not short I am me
I love to laugh I love to dance
I love the simplest things in life
I love music that fits my moods
I love the outdoors especially running in the snow
Fast cars, motorbikes, a train, a plane or two
I love to see people smile
What do you love
It's your turn to add your piece down below.

I WOULD

I would swap you out for a bag of chips and
    a cold beer
I would swap you out and I would not care
I would swap you out and dry my tears
I would swap you out if you get on my last nerves
I would swap you out if you follow me about
I would swap you out if you do not clear your plate,
Mop the floor, make the bed
I would swap you out if you do not wash your hair
I would swap you out if you lay around all day
I would swap you out if you fail to take me out
    on a date
I would swap you out if your eyes gaze in a
    different direction
I would swap you out time and time again.

LAZINESS

Laziness don't cut it for me
Laziness cannot make a cup of tea
Laziness relies on everyone else
Laziness don't work to eat, they just rest
Laziness can become a disease
Laziness is out of reach
Laziness cannot see beyond their eyelid
Laziness is plain and simple a burden to the land
They live on the people that they meet.

DREAM

One can dream of many things
But in reality it's just a dream
One can dream ahead of time
And forget the place they are at
One can dream of paradise or
        swimming with dolphins
One can dream of going to space or
        becoming an astronaut
One can dream of having a perfect wedding
Along with a perfect life

But in the end it's only a dream if you do not
        try to achieve it
A dream is just a dream. So don't just sit and dream
Do something about it you won't know unless
        you try
So why dream the impossible when you can
        live a realistic life.

TIME

Is there a time in your life when you say
    enough is enough
Is there a time in your life when you say sod it
    enough is enough
Is there a time in your life when you look at yourself
    and say enough is enough
Is there a time in your life when you have to give up
    on a friendship
And say enough is enough
Is there a time when you will wake up and say
    enough is enough
Has that time come yet? "No", don't worry, it will.

LOVE AND LIKE

You can love as many people but to find that special
        somebody that you like
Who captured the inner core of your heart
That somebody who sets your world apart
That somebody who makes you feel wow
As if you were looking at the stars in the sky
That someone who lights up your smile
Just like when you see the rising of the sun

Whenever you find that special someone
Please hold them close and never let them go

HAVE YOU EVER

Have you ever jumped out of bed and shouted,
    "Hell no!"
I cannot live this way, time to take action,
    that's as far as you got
For there is no plan in place – impulse is a great
    thing if it's done at the right time
and place – you may disagree. But do I care,
    not really
Oh well back to bed I will try again tomorrow.

REGRETS

I regret the time I met you
I regret the time I said I do
I regret the time I listened to your lies
I regret the tears I cried
I regret not listening to passers-by
I regret not hearing my inner voice
I regret the day I thought the earth stood still
I regret letting you into my world
I regret the years I spent trying to teach you things
I regret so many things in life
But most of all I regret ever knowing you.

NO REGRETS

I don't regret the things I say
I don't regret knowing you
I don't regret the choice I made
I don't regret the day I met you
I don't regret the time I spent with you
I don't regret the things I did for you
I don't regret not having to choose
There are many things I don't regret
But most importantly I don't regret saying I do.

ARE YOU KIDDING ME

Are you kidding me, are you for real
Just like that no worry, no emotion
You just going to leave me standing here
"What?" You are bouncing to where?
You are so heartless you don't care
You are trading me for what looks like something
    on stilts
Or is that a witch without a broomstick
Am I such a burden
"What!" who has an allergy, why not pop two pills
I cannot believe it, I thought you loved me, I
    thought you liked me
I gave you the best years, why did you rescue me in
    the first place
You should have left me at my own faith
You used me to gain the chick that looks like a
    witch on stilts

Now you have taken me to the side of the road and
        left me in the rain
I should have bitten your ankle but I am too tame
Go on drive away – look he did not even look back
"Oh man!" there is no shelter from the rain what
        do I do now?

HIM TO HER

I promise to see you through the hard times
But I won't go to jail
I promise to always be by your side
But not in the grave
I promise to keep you warm throughout the winter
Here, take my sleeping bag
I promise not to be angry when you crash the car
It's your mother-in-law.

HER TO HIM

I promise not to cook
I promise not to clean
I promise not to run up the bills or spend your cash
I promise not to always smile
I promise not to always be positive
Even if it pains me
I promise to leave your sorry ass behind
I am out of here. Free at last.

I AM THINKING

I want you to know this
Who me
I want you to know this
What
I want you to know this
What is it
I want you to know this
Come on what is it
I want you to know this
Come on out with it
I want you to know this
The suspense what is it
I want you to know this
Now you are making me angry
What is it I am losing my mind

I want you to know this
What is it
OK here it is I am thinking we should split
I can see you have no patience, for I was thinking
Why you little bleep bleep bleep
No need for that, for I was thinking how long will it
Take for you to react
Goodbye.

WHAT IS IT

You satisfied my endless desire
Your beauty there is so much to admire
When the light shines on you how my mouth drools
A dribble or two runs down my chin
Should I satisfy my craving

You are beautiful and so delicious
Let me close back the fridge, you stay there and chill
Morning has risen let me go cut a slice
Mercy me, who ate my cake and only left me the
Cherry on the plate?

NARCISSISTIC

How you exploit others without guilt or shame
How dare you need constant praise and admiration
Your love comes with a high price
You talk a good game
Everyone believes what you say
You have no empathy for anyone or anything
You disregard the feelings of others
You are not capable to walk in their shoes
A narcissistic life is so hard to believe
For in their perfect world they come first
It's a sad state of affairs
Yet they will not get the help they need
For they do not believe they have that
        dangerous disease.

DON'T JUST SAY IT

Show me how much you love me
Swim to the bottom of the sea
Find a pearl and bring it back to me
If a mermaid should catch you
Pretend you don't know me

Show me how much you care
Wipe my feet wash my hair
Wipe the part of me that I cannot reach
My back of course – what did you think I meant
Show me how much you like me
Buy me the biggest and sweetest meal
Cut my steak, feed me.

I SEE

I show you how much I care
I'll send you back to the sea
I show you how much I care
I won't wash your feet or wash your hair
Not even where you cannot reach
I show you how much I like you
I won't buy the biggest sweetest meal
Or even cut your steak

Why won't you please me
Because you are very greedy and your laziness
Don't cut it for me.

IF I

If I had to sing you a lullaby
I'd sing you one in my name
If I had to climb the tallest tree
I'd do it for my cat is stuck up there
If I had to run a marathon I'd do it for fame
You will do all that for you
No.
Don't worry you'll get to watch. You might
        learn something
For the world does not revolve around you
This is my world, welcome to my game.

FRIENDS TALKING

Well mate, tell us your story
A man like me has high standards
Picky I am, looks are on the top of my romance list

So here I am having lunch at a prestigious restaurant
I must confess, overpriced, but that's the price
        you pay
If you want to impress

As I read the menu I glance up to take a sip of
        my wine
In she walks
Her hair black as the dark night
The bright red lipstick complements her skin

As the waiter shows her to her seat, she looks over
        at me and smiles
I quickly avert my eyes, pretend to be shy

I make a little hole in the menus to watch her
        from my seat
She checks the time and orders a glass of wine

I order my meal, when it arrives I started to eat
I then glance up at her
I see a sad look on her face
I finish my meal, I did not want to waste it
For there was not much on the plate in the
        first place
For the price I pay, two bites and it's gone

I write a message on the napkin and ask the waiter
To pass it on to her
He takes it over on a silver tray
She receives it, looks at me and smiles
Her expression changes as she reads the note
She then blows her nose on the napkin and sends it
        right back to me
I am horrified

I ask the waiter to dispose of it and get me my bill
The cheeky waiter charges me for the napkin as well

I was so upset
I settled the bill – no tip – and as I was walking past
I pulled off her wig and took it with me
I did not look back
OK just a quick glance, the waiter was covering her
    head with a napkin

Hahaha (friends laughing)
Why are you all laughing, it was embarrassing
    for me

Really but you ended it so meanly
Well, the note I wrote was kind

Really, what was in this note?
Oh, by the way, here comes a friend of ours
Hahaha (friends laugh)

You rotters, you set me up

I think this is the part where you run.
It's payback time.

HOW TIME HAS DRASTICALLY CHANGED

We are told there was a time when men were men
    and women were women
You know men dressed in bowler hats or whatever
    hats of their choice
And fine suits
And the ladies too, along with their fine
    modest dresses
No hair out of place

They would both sip tea out of the best Chinaware
With their little pinky finger on display

Gentlemen would tilt their hats as they walked by
Giving one another that respect

A businessman's handshake was as good as his word
Ladies walking upright with style and grace
Taking a lady on a date, a gentleman would bring
        her a small gesture
She would giggle how sweet
He would ensure she was home on time
        never too late
Oh how time has come a long way

Forward to our time
Not much can be said
Anything goes
Everyone can dress the same no boundaries
It's a popularity contest.

I too can play if I choose to

I know long ago women fought for equal rights
Now we are fighting for the men to get off their
        lazy asses and do some work
Many men have taken a back seat

Just look at the amount of work that needs
        to be done

Fences needs repairing, grass needs cutting,
     house needs painting
A man's castle should be looking crisp
Instead it is fighting for the will to stay upright

Let's check in
You leave the house to get provisions for the family
He has promised to get the work done
A shopping list of things you have left

But as you step out that door he watches through
     the window as you walk away
Shopping basket in hand,
Of course, he could take you in the car but then
     the work would not get done

The sun is shining, the neighbours have fired up
     their BBQ
The smell penetrates the air

Cricket is about to start, yep he is off
Chair slicked back, beer in the bucket chilling
TV out on the lawn on displays
I guess no work will be done today

You came home tired of dragging that old
        shopping basket
A long way to home, bus broke down

To your surprise the grass was cut, the fence
Was mended, there he is relaxing
So everything that you were thinking
Now you feel bad, so you make him his
        favourite meal
As he sits and watches the cricket
You will not nag

That night when you went to bed, treat night
A knock at the door

A tall slim man with hair slicked back gave a smile
Yep, he came to drop the change off
You inquired of this change and as the
        man explained
You could feel your anger ablaze

You thanked the man and said nothing else
You then checked the camera
And reclined back in bed

The next evening he arrived home
Only to find you relaxing in bed
"Darling," he said, "why is there a man in
    my kitchen
"And you are in bed?"

A response he did get
You thought since you like others to do your work
Why not get him to do the rest
So your dinner he will cook, your wife
    he will service
Don't forget to give him a large tip
Now please do not disturb
For I am watching the race

You'd think he just had a heart attack.
Or did he just faint?

No peeps
Nothing happened between the man
And you
For it was your plan
Just a payback for your man's laziness.
Hahaha hahaha
A lesson he will learn.

WHAT WOULD YOU SAY

So you want to take this next step
Then the *I do* a commitment not to be taken likely
You will come across a lot of bumps along the way
How you deal with them will test your strengths
Your love for one another

For as God put the marriage arrangements in place
He did not say it was going to be easy
Let not jealousy or unreasonableness
And bad minded people tear you apart

Let your words be gracious, seasoned with salt
Always set in your calendar time for each other
You may have different hobbies or interests
But find something that you both like and
        do together

Remember not all men like to shop with
        their partner
But yet they do it even if it means keeping the peace
So do the same for him if asked

Don't take today's disagreement into tomorrow
Or the day after
If there is a crack, fix it before it become unfixable
For then everyone will be coming with their
        branded plaster
In other words their own opinion
Helpful as they may try to be
Confusion it will bring
Get to know each other's weakness and be their
        strengths

One last thing
You probably will get moaning and groaning
Am I too fat in this?
Is my hair going thin
I have no clothes to wear
Just turn and hold him and say
(Oh remember let your words be gracious)
Baby you look as good today as the day
        I married you

If that doesn't work then I can't help you —
        best read the fine print

That says for better or for worse.

I CAN AND I CAN'T
V
I WILL DO, I CAN DO

I can't say I am thrilled to see you
You bring me nothing but indigestion
I can't say I am longing to see you
You only bring pain and worry to my life

I can't say I am happy to see you
You only make me lose my appetite
Where is this going
I don't know, I thought it rhymed so I thought
     I would go along with it

I can't say I forgive you for you will only do it again
One of your favourite things to say is I can't
Along with I won't, I cannot, I will not
These I don't want to know, they are so annoying

I will do, I can do, I am going to do,
But these can hang around with me all the time

TOO MAD TO TALK TO

If I have nine lives and you take one
How much me have left

Now let me see, you have nine lives and me take one
How much you have left
Come on what's the answer
Wait I am thinking

Twenty-four hours later him still a thinking
You have nine lives me take one
But which one did I take
I don't know which one you take

Then how did you know I take it
Because I had nine lives
Well, if you did not see me take it
How can you say I take it, I am no thief

No, no, no I don't really have nine lives I have one
Now you are confusing me
First you say you have nine lives and I took one
But you can't say which one
Now you are saying you have one life
So what happened to the other eight
Oh forget it, let's just play I spy
Who is I spy when did he get here
Forget it.

CRAZY CHAT UP LINES

You hear that?
It's my heart beating like a Cherokee drum
        when I am near you.
Response: step back
You look so sweet you could sweeten my tea
Response: sorry I am only into coffee
Wow you smell so nice what you wearing –
        Chinese five spice?
Response: everyday seasoning

You are the moon I am the sun, how about it
Response: sorry you are too hot for me
Hey come over here and let me show you my engine
Response: what a load of junk
I am Batman, you want to be my Robin?
Response: sorry I love the joker

I will fall down a thousand flights of stairs for you
Response: on the way down knock some sense
        into your head
I am sweeter than sugar tastier than honey,
        you want to try me
Response: diabetes is not my style
Do you hear that? It's the sound of my belly rolling,
        you care to join me for dinner?
Response: no thanks, I am vegetarian

You stole my heart from afar
Response: really, and you are still alive
Your voice is like music to my ears
Response: what did you say?
You give me ingestion when I think of you
Response: you give me diarrhoea –
        there, we are even
Evol you are to me, evol in every way
Response: I will buy you a dictionary.
Look at me, what's there not to like?
Response: you

I can be your first your second or your last
Just put me where you want me
Response: anyone got a rocket
Look deep into my eyes, what do you see?
Response: wait, let me get the torch
I am the cherry in your pie, the cream in your coffee
Response: someone please get me a straitjacket.

THOSE WE LOVED
AND LOST

I lay awake hoping not to get that knock at the door
    or that phone call
Telling me what I don't want to hear,
For as you pack your loved one's bag and
    kiss them goodbye
Just for that day or more
We look forward to welcoming them back
That very evening or later down the years

But today my worst fear arises
There it is, a knock on the door
The kind of knock that makes your stomach sink
As I slowly make my way to the door praying
    please God let it not be
But, yes. It is to be
One look at the officer's face I feel my knees
    give way

The officer catches me before my body hits the floor
I am so sorry, he says, missing in action
A lump comes to my throat as I try to tell myself
Only missing in action, there is hope
I keep the candle flame of love close to my
        beating heart
For if it were to be extinguished then that will be
        the end of me
I write a letter every week hoping for some news
Hoping my letters will find him wherever he may be

But hope never came.
I am now 85 years old and still holding on to hope
But still nothing, is hope not an assured thing?
All these years waiting as tears stream down my face
Still missing in action, that's all they could say

Over time many suitors approach me
But I turn them away, still waiting for hope

At last a parcel comes
All that I have written is inside a box
Tied with my favourite colours
And a tulip, my favourite flower
Hope promises to return
Hope and faith is the nickname we gave to
        each other
This was part of our promise to each other during
        our wedding vows
He was hope, I was faith
Hope and faith
As I open the box there inside is a note
It just simply says, my dearest faith keep hope alive,
        see you on the other side.

Where are you now

Are you in heaven looking down watching my
        daily routine
Are you in hell, a place that some believe to exist,
        screaming out my name?
Perhaps you are a bird hovering about or are you
        a tree that is blowing
Its leaves as I pass by

There are many interpretations as to where you are
    after you die
But for me you are asleep, a place of rest
Awaiting like the man Job to hear your name called
From the God above, awakening you will be soon
In a world of peace and security
That is where I believe we will one day meet
Until then rest in peace.

FROM ME TO YOU

I comfort you with the comfort I received from God
I comfort you with the prayer I am taught through
    Jesus Christ
I comfort you with the love of friendship
Who will comfort the comforter
Who will rise and give a smile
Who will let you know that things are going
    to be alright?
For the God above give with love so I give back
    in gratitude.

A PAIN SO GREAT

The pain of losing a child is far greater than one
    can imagine
Yet they say time is a great healer
But the pain a parent feels you cannot compare to
    a toothache
Or a root canal

So how would one describe a pain of a parent?
I cannot describe it nor would I want to
For just thinking about it has stirred up what was
    once put to sleep
For when a child is no more half if not all
Of that parent's heart, an inner soul has gone
    with them

They are a thorn between living and dying
It may seem a choice one does not want to make
But for some it's not an impossible choice
For a parent's love is unconditional lasting love.

THE FORTUNATE TO
THE UNFORTUNATE

Little child rise and smile it's the start of a new day
Your bag is packed come comb your hair
Breakfast is on the table, plenty of choices today
Take your pick, whatever it is I can make it
For school is a long day, bellyful you must be.

ON THE OTHER SIDE

Little child come now, get up plenty of work
    to be done
Go fetch the water, make sure the bucket is full
    this time
No breakfast today, hurry now the school bell
    will soon ring
Don't want you to be late

Here, sip a cup of hot water to warm your belly up
May God bless your day

But grandma, it would have been better if God bless
    me with some breakfast
Did you give thanks for yesterday's supper?
No Grandma!
Child no matter how poor or rich one is
    we give thanks
For today we will eat but no one knows
    about tomorrow
Take this slice of bread and off you go.

TO DO OR NOT TO DO

I follow the crowd to a point then I stop and
	turn right back
Shall we start again
Growing up I was taught to think big
I go to bed thinking big dreaming big

Yet I am only 4 feet 3, does that seem big to you?
For the shoes you wear cannot fit me nor the
	clothes you wear
Or the house you have, I need a map to find my
	way around it
So I stop to ask myself, why am I following
	the crowd?
I don't need to think big, I just need to find
	what suits me.

A DIFFERENT KIND
OF GENERATION

They know how to drink and smoke
Cuss whenever they don't get their way
This planet has evolved into a huge playground
For them to be whatever they choose to be

Hard work is not their priority
Work two hours and they want a break
They don't know what it's like to pay a bill,
      they don't care
What does a pint of milk cost, no doubt
      they will guess
Video games and designer shoes is all that they
      want to know

Horror awaits them as they reach adulthood
Realisation hits them hard
So they pop two pills to forget
Where are they now, it's a crying shame.

TANTRUM BOY
VERSUS
MAN

Why can't I make my own decision?
Why can't I smoke?
Why can't I drink beer?
Why can't I break gas and not say oops!
Why can't I sleep in my clothes so I don't have
    to get dressed?
Why do I have to have a bath every day?
Why can't I stay up late?
STOP!!! Enough

You are not yet old enough to make the
    right decisions
You are not old enough to smoke
I would not want you to do that, it's bad
    for your health
You are not old enough to drink, I would not
    recommend it
You can break gas, it's natural for the body
But it's good manners to say excuse me when
    in company

You cannot sleep in your clothes
You will crease them
You need to wash or else you will stink
And you will get teased

You need good sleep, it's better for your mind
    and body
Plus your eyeballs will complain

(He scratches his head looking puzzled)

But, but uncle Harry does them all, he said that's
What being a man is

Well, you are only seven
And your uncle is a buffoon.

HELLO FRIEND

Just started a new job
Met a beautiful young man
I use the term beautiful
For a man can be handsome
But his beauty is within
As I was saying
Eyes as clear as the Mediterranean waters,
     a smile that can melt ice
His skin tone, how would one describe it?
I am still thinking
Dressed in a grey suit with open shirt,
     what a diamond
As he opened his mouth to speak, a slight accent
I did detect
Neither short nor tall, just right, so the girls don't
     have to tip toe, who is this mystery guy?
He introduced himself with a firm handshake
Hi, I am … let's just leave his name out
His cheeks became powder pink as he smiled a
     little embarrassed, going all shy
Excuse me while I nip outside for some fresh air,
     you are making me all hot, he said

What happened next?
He returned walking up two flights of stairs
Carrying a hot tray trying not to let it spill on
    his suit
While many walked on by, he saw there was a
    need to help, he did not think twice
Was he worried about getting his suit spoilt?
So I thank him with a grateful smile
What else?
I don't know, I just focused on my work
He went off to find his friends
Oh man!!! You always do that. Get us to a point
    and then pop the balloon.

THEIR EYES SEE

Friends notice when things are not right
Word does not have to speak to know things are
     going the way it should be.

Love comes easy to some, love can be divine
In many ways
But true love takes long to find, look at both
     your age

When you find this love, it comes with its ups
        and downs
It will test you beyond your limit
To the point of letting it go
But knowing each other's weakness can strengthen
        you both, iron sharpen iron
That's love.
Fight for it, don't give up
This is real love so it will test you
Remember what love is: patience. It endures
        all things
Give up on love, not only hurt yourself but
        hurt each other
You will forever question yourself, did I do right,
        did I act on emotions or did I give it
        real thought

A first time parent has a child not knowing what
        really to expect but then challenges arise
They begin to regret and so name and finger
        pointing commence.
Now they are apart leaving one to cope alone
And someone else to come along to try and mend
        that broken heart
But still the damage is done, they begin to second
        guess themselves
Never to gain trust and find happiness.

You have both built a memory of happy times
visiting places that you both did not have time for
        before enjoying the scenery
Now the honeymoon period is over
The reality of the next step has drawn close
But whatever is the issue
Please sort it out

There is nothing that is cracked or broken that
        cannot be fixed
With a lot of TLC (tender loving care)
Whatever it is, face it, don't be afraid
Keep impulsive emotions out
And if it is within him, I say to him
Fix it, put pride aside, don't say it's a man thing
We all are built differently in some things
But emotions run deep within

Two oceans apart yet look how you both find
        each other, who would have thought
Don't overthink it
You are both worth fighting for

Love unfailing love, no one said it would be easy
Some things are worth fighting for
Boy see your girl
Girl see your boy …
Fix it.

FATHERS WHAT HAVE YOU DONE

The universe has a way of putting ones together and
        holding them so tight
But on the flip side, it can break you apart
A dad is for life not just for Christmas or birth
Whether they play a big part or not
They are out there somewhere

Now and then looking back and wondering how
　　you are doing
But never taking an active part
A father wants to enjoy life, enjoy what the universe
　　has to offer
Then run away from the responsibility
Of taking care of what he has added to this world
Only to find another host and start the process
　　all over again now it has become a
　　production line
Yet he cannot cope
He just keeps adding to the universe
Until the universe has had enough
And sends his world crashing down
Children born to a man a father look back now
But it's too late, the universe has other plans
Your greed and selfish behaviour have cost you
What you want to value most in life
It's too late, the universe has closed the door
Now you are all alone.

BRAIN

It's sad to see the state of one's brain
A beautiful brain that you were born with
A brain that can take you far, it has no limit
It was created to live for ever
Take care of it and it will take care of you
Your brain is like food to the belly,
      be careful of what you put in it.

DADDY, DADDY

One day you were here, now you are gone
The hand that held me as a mere baby
You saw my first smile, you dropped a tear
You watched me grow, you stayed quite near
My first bike you taught me how to ride
I fell once or twice
You picked me up and give me a warm hug
And brightened up my smile
Back on my bike I rode with such pride
For my daddy was there right by my side
Look daddy, I am riding
Yes, that's my girl, he shouted proudly
Pointing his finger at me with a great big smile
People passing by stopped to look

I got ice cream that day as a treat
It was so big I had to use both hands to hold it
With some help from my dad
As he licked the corner of my ice cream before it
       could melt in my lap

As I grew, I did not understand
What did I do wrong?
He began to drift away, I did not recognise
My daddy, I guess life had other plans
For he would walk the streets like a mad man
I was hopeless to help
When there was a window I could connect
For that very moment it was precious
But then that sad look in his eyes, he has was once
    again pulled from my arms
Now locked behind bars for a crime he did commit,
    he tried to get help but his willpower kept
    slipping away for bad people played a part
A phone call now and then I would get

He did so much wrong in his life
Family he did hurt, friends turned their backs
Bullying is what I got, my school days become a
  nightmare, all because my daddy went astray
Whatever it was that made his head become sick,
  the answer I did not get
For family tried to protect my innocence
Now my dad is laid to rest
Behind bars he fell asleep, I could not understand, I
  cried but not for long
As I cannot accept that he is gone
But let me say this on his behalf
So sorry for all the hurt he has caused
Some hurt goes beyond repair
I kid you not
Please find it in your heart to forgive him
For his head was not where it should be
Certain family had given up on him
But never truly understood the pain that was eating
  up inside of him
He reached out one last time crying for help
But only to find it was too late
That family door was finally closed.

R.I.P. Your pain is ended.

LAZY JANCRO

You good for nothing Jancro
Are you addressing me mongoose
Way rat da
Him here hiding under the leaves
Me have no business with you Jancro
So no eat me please
Well me have bone to pick with you Jancro
For me catch me meat when sun hat
Whiles you settle under the mango tree
Laughing at me

Me run inner Bush to bring back sweet potato
Now you say you no thief me meat
But is not that me chicken bone you use
        to clean your beak.
Settle yourself mongoose, plenty more treats
        in the farmer's
Yard, send rat go open the cage him ugly face
        will scare the chicken
Then we all can have a feast
Come rat go climb
Mongoose tell Jancro not to eat me
Go on rat him na go eat you
Him only love dead things that can't fight back.
        Him one lazy Jancro.

[Look out for Jancro and his friends
Coming soon, next edition ...]